THE LADY OR THE TIGER
THE YOUNG MAN MUST CHOOSE

Linda Costarella

Published in December 2016

DEDICATION

To my husband and son for their love and support

CONTENTS

1
PROLOGUE

The short story *The Lady, or the Tiger?* published by Frank R. Stockton in 1882 inspired this book. In Stockton's story, a semi-barbaric[1] king had built an arena for a very specific purpose: to conduct games of chance that would determine the innocence or guilt of individuals who he had put on trial for some wrongdoing.

The accused would walk into the arena and stand before two doors. Behind one stood a hungry tiger in an open cage. If he opened that door, the king presumed him guilty, and the accused would be devoured. Behind the other waited a beautiful lady. If the man opened that door, he was presumed innocent. Whether he was already married or loved someone else, the victim would be forced to marry the lady he had just met. The king did whatever pleased his fancy, and his system of justice entertained him greatly.

---

1   **semi-** a prefix meaning *half*
     barbaric (adj) uncivilized, primitive

Frank R. Stockton

In Stockton's story, the accused was a young courtier who had dared to have an affair with the king's daughter. The king threw the man in jail, and arranged for him to enter the arena to make a choice that would determine his innocence or guilt.

This is the story of what happened after the young man entered the arena...

2
AT THE ARENA

Two prison guards led the young man out of the dungeon and down the long corridor of the old stone castle. As he stepped through the door, he suddenly found himself squinting and turning his head down away from the light. *I've been in that prison for so long, my eyes are not used to the daylight anymore,* he thought. *Oh... how I have longed to breathe the fresh air and feel the sun's warmth.*

For the last few weeks, the young man had been imprisoned in a cold, dark dungeon. Day and night looked exactly the same in the small, stuffy cell. Only by his instincts could the young man sense the passing of time. Now out of the darkness, his eyes adjusted to the light and he felt invigorated by the sun's rays shining between the clouds on the cool summer day. *I don't care what lies ahead. This feels good right now.*

The man was certain that the two burly[2] prison guards were leading him straight to the king's arena; he had anticipated this moment since the day of his arrest. It was known throughout the land that the king had the amphitheater built for this very purpose, to determine the innocence or guilt of prisoners accused of crimes.

The alleged crime that the young man had been accused of committing was one of love. He was a commoner who had dared to have a relationship with the lovely young princess – the king's only daughter.

---

2   **burly** (adj) large in bodily size; stout

The young man and the princess had met in secret for many months. However, the king eventually learned of their relationship from a servant who had seen them together, and now the young man would pay a severe price for his serious lack of judgment.

My heart is pounding like a drum, the young man thought as the guards led him with long, sure strides. *I know what is going to happen next.*

He had no doubt that he would soon be forced to choose between two doors, and that each one concealed an option meant to separate him from the beautiful princess once and for all. The man knew the princess well. She was shrewd, and had a fiercely determined nature similar to that of her own father. She also tended a bit toward jealousy, he thought, remembering the slight pout on her lips upon seeing him engage in a few words of innocent conversation with a female servant.

Having an abundance of time in the dungeon to contemplate his situation, the young man had convinced himself of three things: that the princess would try to uncover the secret of the doors, that she would succeed in her efforts, and that she would attempt to lead him to one door or the other.

I cannot decide which fate she would choose for me. After all, she is not part of either choice. In response to his own proclamation of love, the princess had told him that she loved him dearly. *It could not have been easy for her to imagine what might await me behind either door.*

The young man's mind began to race. *Would she send me to the path that would lead to my marriage to another woman, or to the one that would lead to my death? I just don't know.*

Chilled by the cool air, a marked difference from his stifling[3] cell, the man shivered as the guards led him toward the arena. The moment that he had envisioned for weeks was now before him.

3   **stifling** (adj) stuffy, muggy, airless

The spectators rose to their feet and cheered as he entered the arena, anticipating great entertainment when he made the choice that would forever alter the course of his life. He saw the two identical doors, then scanned the arena, deafened by the noise from the crowd, a stark contrast from the torturing silence of the dungeon.

Now, seeing the king seated upon his grand throne with his daughter to his right, the man looked away, using his forearm to wipe the sweat from his brow. He took a deep breath, exhaled slowly, then turned toward them again. His gaze fell on the princess momentarily. Their eyes met, and she gestured with a slight movement of her right hand. He looked away immediately. *There is no mistaking her intention; she gave me a signal to open the door to the right.*

The man looked at the thick, brown doors. The indecision that he had felt during the last few weeks had dissipated.[4]

---

4   **dissipated** (v) dissolved, disintegrated

His heart was heavy, his decision made. If a tiger pounced on him, he would die knowing that he had trusted his lover. If a beautiful lady stood behind the door, he would be married – but not to the woman he loved. *My princess, you are the love of my life.*

The crowd hushed to a whisper as the young man advanced to the right. His heart raced; his throat had gone dry. He moved the heavy latch, and threw open the door.

A beautiful lady stood before him. The crowd exploded in applause, knowing that there would be a festive wedding. The man looked into the eyes of the lady. Then he turned and looked at the lovely princess. *She saved my life; she truly is the love of my life.*

As several young girls carrying small silver pails entered the arena, a priest approached the young man and the beautiful lady, preparing to perform the ceremony. Then musicians entered the amphitheater, and took their places to play their instruments and sing.

The young man, happy to be alive, felt a deep ache in his heart. He had asked for the princess' hand in marriage, but her father – the king – would not accept him because he was a commoner. After today, he would never see her again.

The princess had breathed a sigh of relief when the young man had opened the door on the right. But, as she saw the girls toss rose petals into the air, and heard the performers start to play their music, she found herself choking back tears as she watched the entire ceremony in somber silence. Through all of this, she sensed his love in her heart each time the young man looked up at her.

The king, the Royal Council, and his entire court witnessed the ceremony from their places high in the stands. The king's throne had been set in its usual position, directly opposite the two heavy doors.

For the king, this was a particularly satisfying occasion; one way or the other, he would be rid of the young man – a mere courtier[5] in his palace – who had dared to love his daughter. *She will be better off married to another man, and she will thank me someday,* he thought, looking at his daughter's tearful face. *I have her future heirs to consider, after all, and they will not be fathered by a mere peasant in my kingdom.*

5   **courtier** (n) a person who is part of a ruler's court, who lives with the ruler and depends on him for a living

3
JUST ONE NIGHT

After the wedding, two tall royal guards accompanied by a stout,[6] middle-aged gentleman ushered the newlyweds out of the arena. The gentleman then led the groom to a room on the ground floor of the palace. The room had a single window which looked out onto the vast land at the back of the castle.

"Your bride will be with you momentarily," the gentleman stated, as he closed the door behind him. The young man looked out the window. *I have lost my princess forever. I don't know how I'm going to live without her.* The king's orders had been clear: the groom would spend one night with his new bride, after which the two of them would leave the palace together, never to return again.

The door creaked and slowly opened. The young man sighed, and turned toward the door. His jaw dropped when he saw his lover, the princess, standing in the doorway.

---

6   **stout** (adj) heavy, portly

"What? But…how?" he asked.

She looked up at him with the trace of a smile. "Are you disappointed, my dear?" she asked.

"My princess, how did you manage…?" he stammered,[7] taking her hand.

---

7   **stammer** (v) to speak with involuntary breaks and pauses

"I gave her an heirloom[8] – my grandmother's gold necklace – for agreeing to change places with me. She promised to say nothing of our arrangement, and has already left the palace."

"But she and I were married, my princess. You saw the ceremony yourself."

"Yes, it is true, my dear, that I did witness the ceremony. We will deal with that matter at a later date."

"But what will happen tomorrow? The lady and I were supposed to be escorted from the palace together, never to return again."

"We will leave tonight instead. In an hour we will be taken to a house by the woods where we will never be found."

---

8   **heirloom** (n) valuable treasure

"Never in my wildest dreams could I imagine such a plan, my princess," the young man said as he gently touched her cheek.

"You never answered my question, my dear. Are you disappointed?"

The young man embraced the princess, kissing her forehead, her cheek, and finally her lips. "Please believe me, my princess. Oh, to be alive and with the woman I love... Today, I am the happiest man in the world."

The princess smiled. "It pleases me to hear you say that," she replied.

"Haven't I asked you to marry me a hundred times before? I feel no differently now."

"Yes, a hundred times before, my dear, and married we would be if my father had not interfered. I love my father; but though he is king, I will be the one who will choose my husband."

The man recalled the king's exact words when he had asked for his daughter's hand in marriage. "We are royalty," the king had declared. "Royal blood is royal blood. Royalty is born to royalty. You are a commoner, young man, and as such, you cannot marry someone of my daughter's status. You must find a wife who is suitable for you. My daughter will not marry you."

Though the king's reply had been expected, the words stung. *I will remember His Majesty's words for the rest of my life. The lovely princess has owned my heart since the day I first saw her. I can't change that any more than I can change the fact that I was born to a family of commoners. God has blessed me because my princess loves me.*

Moonbeams reflected off a nearby lake, and stars danced in the sky. The young man and the princess enjoyed each other's company as they anxiously awaited the arrival of the person who would lead them to safety.

The princess remembered the day she had first seen the young man; he was brought to the palace to help maintain the gardens and the courtyards. She had been walking outside as usual, enjoying the beautiful landscape.

At that moment, their eyes met. Though they did not speak that first day, future walks in the garden brought them together again and again. "I like working outdoors very much," she remembered him saying. In reality, it was her beauty that he was admiring, not the beauty of the landscape.

As time passed, the young man and the princess got to know each other more and more. They found ways to meet where they could be alone, although for periods of time that were far too brief.

Almost a year had passed. *I know he has just been married to someone else,* she thought, *but I pray that someday we will marry and spend the rest of our lives together.*

A grandfather clock in the hallway chimed at one o'clock in the morning. Soon, the young man heard three taps at the door. He turned toward the door, but the princess had already opened it.

The same middle-aged man who had escorted him to the room stood in the doorway. "This is my father's steward,"[9] the princess stated. "He has known me since the day I was born."

---

9   **steward** (n) a person who manages the daily affairs of the castle, including its finances, and is in charge of the servants

"It is time," the steward said. "Your father will be looking for you soon."

The steward silently ushered the young couple down a small hallway, through a back door, and into a small, black carriage where a horseman drove them away. He watched them go down the rugged road until the clip-clop of the horses' trot became imperceptible.[10]

---

10   **imperceptible** (adj) undetectable

4
THE SEARCH IS ON

In the morning, the king sat at the large wooden table in the great hall. While he waited for his breakfast to be served, he inquired about his daughter. A member of his court reported what the steward had told him: "She was not feeling well and decided to sleep late this morning, Sire."

"Very well," the king said, "I will have a talk with her later." He enjoyed a large breakfast and dozed in his favorite chair, pleased that the young man had married someone other than his daughter, and that he had left his kingdom once and for all.

Later the king awakened. He busied himself with members of his Royal Council who had come to see him about some commoners' requests. *Such trivial matters,* he thought, as he discussed them with the Council in the great hall. Then he inquired once again as to the well-being of his daughter.

The steward reported to the king: "She is not feeling well. Still indisposed,[11] Sire."

"Still? I wonder if she is mourning[12] her loss. I must speak with her immediately."

The king went to his daughter's room, and knocked on the door. Receiving no answer, he entered the empty room. "My word," he said. "What has happened? Where is my dear daughter?"

---

11   **indisposed** (adj) unwilling, disinclined, reluctant, under the weather

12   **mourn** (v) to feel or express sorrow or grief

"I do not know, Sire. Perhaps she went for a walk," the steward replied, avoiding eye contact with the king.

The king looked in his daughter's wardrobe; her jewels and some of her clothes were gone. The king raised his eyebrows, then wrinkled them as he angrily regarded his steward. "What is the meaning of this? What has transpired[13]?" he asked.

---

13   **transpire** (v) to occur; happen; take place

"I do not know, Sire. I am sorry. I am not aware of the princess' whereabouts," the steward replied, shifting from one foot to the other.

"Where is that young man? I must see him immediately."

"He and his new wife have already left the palace as you had commanded," the steward said, his voice quivering[14] as he spoke.

"I do not believe you. What in God's name is going on here? Where is my daughter? I must find her."

The king summoned his constable,[15] and commanded the tall, broad-shouldered man to alert all palace guards of his order to begin searching for the princess.

Later that day, the king met an older woman who had been a loyal servant in the palace for many years. "Have you seen my daughter?" he asked.

---

14   **quiver** (v) to shake with a slight but rapid motion; to tremble
15   **constable** (n) the commander of all armed forces in the kingdom

"No, Your Highness," she responded, blood rushing to her cheeks. "I have not seen her."

"And what about the new bride? You witnessed the ceremony yesterday. Have you seen her?"

"Not since she left last night, Your Highness," the woman replied, suddenly raising her hand to her lips, gasping in embarrassment.

"Last night? And just where did she go last night, may I ask?"

"Oh... well, Sire... I am not quite sure," the older woman responded, trembling slightly, her right hand still pressed to her lips.

The king approached the woman, his head stopping inches from her face. His voice was low and determined. "Tell me where the bride has gone, or I will be forced to have the information pried from you in a way that I assure you will be most unpleasant."

The older woman froze in place, her hands on her cheeks as the king spoke. Then she stammered, "She... she left the kingdom without the young man. The princess gave her a magnificent necklace so that she would leave the kingdom without her new husband."

The steward, who had been roaming the castle, entered the great hall and saw the agitated king pacing as the older woman stood off to one side shaking. The king bellowed, "That bride has defied me. No one will make a fool of me and live to tell about it. I will find my daughter and that scoundrel.[16] He will enter the arena a second time, for an even more delightful game of chance, for behind one door will be a fierce tiger, and behind the other will be another tiger, hungrier and fiercer still. Then we will see if he will be able to choose the correct door. And that bride who has fled without her husband will be very sorry that she has undermined[17] me. I will have that necklace wrapped around her scrawny little neck."

16   **scoundrel** (n) a person who is a rascal or a villain
17   **undermine** (v) challenge, undercut, weaken

"Your Majesty, you cannot be serious," said his steward.

"Oh, I am quite serious. As for my lovely daughter... we must have a long talk. I have been far too lenient[18] with her. She will not be permitted to take any man of her choosing. She will return to the palace and marry whomever I say she will marry. In fact, I have the perfect suitor in mind; and unfortunately for her, she will be miserable when she

18   **lenient** (adj) tolerant, permissive, indulgent

discovers his identity. She will be punished for plotting behind my back. She must never, ever disobey me again."

A servant had come to the door to announce the arrival of the Chancellor of the Royal Council. His Highness waved his hand to welcome the tall, heavy-set man, and the visitor entered the room. The chancellor, who had always been on relatively good terms with the king, soon understood the reason for the king's displeasure. Since the king had previously talked about his plan for his daughter to marry a man of her status, His Majesty's position in this matter did not surprise him.

Hesitant to involve himself in personal matters involving the king, the chancellor thought it best to remain silent. However, the king asked for his comment.

"Your Highness, all three have left your kingdom," the chancellor stated. "Perhaps you should let them be."

"That young man will not marry my daughter! How dare he deceive me after I had made my intentions for her quite clear to him! He will suffer the consequences of his boldness, I assure you. We will soon see the extent of his bravery."

"Your Majesty, I beg you to reconsider," the chancellor implored.[19] "Your daughter's only wish is to be with the man she loves."

"Never! They will all pay for their betrayal."

---

19   **implore** (v) beg, plead

<u>5</u>
THE HOUSE BY THE WOODS

The horseman had left the young man and the princess at the house by the woods with a wooden crate containing food and other supplies. The house was sparsely[20] furnished and quite dusty, having been uninhabited for many months.

---

20   **sparsely** (adv) lightly, sparingly

"It is a cool night," said the young man as he lifted some logs and put them into the fireplace. Soon, the fire crackled and roared as it started to warm the house. He then used the fire to light candles, which he placed around the room. Finally, the man took his lover's hand and led her to the small couch. He put his arm around her shoulder, and they relaxed quietly, exhausted from their long day.

The steward is on our side, the young man thought. *But will he be able to save us, or himself for that matter? He and the king seem to be friends. However, His Majesty will not put up with his disloyalty.*

The princess was struck by the silence in the house, hearing nothing except the crackling of the fire. She thought this very unusual, having spent her entire life in a castle in which dozens of servants and cooks busied themselves with chores throughout the day. *It will take some time for me to get acclimated²¹ to a home like this,* she thought; *the silence is peaceful but a bit eerie.*

"What are you thinking, my princess?" the young man asked, noticing how tired she looked.

---

21   **acclimated** (v) to become accustomed to a new climate or environment; to adapt

She turned toward him, trying to smile through her exhaustion. "Ever since I was a little girl," she recalled, "my father told me that I was special; I was a princess and would live a life beyond the greatest desires of most other girls in the kingdom. Why should that be different now just because I have fallen in love with a commoner? I cannot accept that my father has a right to determine whom I may love."

"But my princess, how did you manage to think of such a plan?" the young man asked, holding her close.

"My father's steward is like my own dear uncle," she replied. "Through him I was able to discover more than my father himself knew – which door hid the lady and which the tiger. There was no choice but to have you open the door behind which stood the lady. I could not have lived with myself had I done anything else."

"What if I had not followed your lead, my princess?" the young man asked, kissing her hand.

"I was certain that you would. We have always trusted each other," she replied, resting her head on his shoulder.

"But, knowing that another woman would step through the doorway, you still saved me. You are an angel."

"Ah, perhaps I am, my dear. But I had no intention of having you spend the rest of your life with that lady, or any other," the princess replied, looping her arm through his.

"Once I discovered the secret of the doors, I devised a plan to have your new bride leave without you. She would have liked to be your wife, believe me, but she liked my gold necklace even more. The fool did not know that you, my love, are more precious than all the gold in the world."

Stunned by what the princess had told him, the young man imagined her father searching for them. He knew that he had to escape the king's wrath;[22] His Highness might be able to forgive his daughter, but he would surely never forgive him.

---

22 **wrath** (n) anger, rage, fury

The young man rose and began to pace back and forth in the small room. "What will we do now?" he asked. "How will we avoid being captured? I have no doubt that your father is looking for us even as we speak."

"Yes, I am sure he is, my dear, and so we must remain hidden." The princess was saddened by the worried look on her lover's face. She rose, moved toward him, and kissed his cheek.

"What you have done amazes me," the young man said, "but, I am afraid that our good luck will not last. When your father finds us, he will surely have me killed." The princess hugged her lover; a tear streamed down her face.

Meanwhile, the king's search for the young man and his daughter continued. He was also determined to find the lady who had made the deal with his daughter.

The members of his court had asked the king to spare the lady's life since she only did what the princess had asked. To that the king replied, "I will have no compassion for that conniving[23] lady; her selfish craving for riches has caused this problem. She will pay for her avarice[24] with her life."

Guards on horseback combed the area for days, hunting for the young man, the princess, and the lady, with the same ferocity that they would hunt animals for slaughter. The constable had ordered the guards to bring the three individuals back to the palace unharmed, but by force if necessary. Finally, several of the king's guards found the house in which the young man and the princess were hiding. Four guards led the couple back to the palace, handling them harshly, as though they were prisoners.

---

23   **conniving** (adj) scheming, deceitful, devious
24   **avarice** (n) insatiable greed for riches; miserly desire to gain and hoard wealth

6
ORDER IN THE COURT

The king was the supreme ruler of the land, and thus had the power to assure that the tiger, which had been confined in his kingdom for years, was feared throughout the countryside. The ferocious animal had been seen in the arena on many occasions when His Highness had conducted his game of chance to determine whether a subject was guilty of one crime or another.

In addition to his peculiar way of administering justice, His Majesty possessed both the power and the quick temper to simply sweep away the life of anyone who irked[25] him. With a single command and a wave of his hand, he would forever banish[26] a poor, unfortunate soul from his place on Earth.

The Royal Council was aware of the king's unique method of imposing justice and had witnessed his trials in the arena many times before. However, the Council had previously advised the king that there should be no more beheadings or other deaths at the whim of royalty, outside of what might take place in the arena every now and then. In fact, the Chancellor of the Royal Council had previously told His Majesty that a king who ordered such deaths was no better than a murdering commoner.

The chancellor had not been surprised when His Highness had dismissed his counsel. "I rule my kingdom as I see fit," the king had said, "and I see no reason to change my ways now. There's nothing wrong with a bit of entertainment every now and then... wouldn't you agree?"

---

25   **irk** (v) bother, annoy
26   **banish** (v) send away; drive out

The king had made known to his entourage[27] the fate of the young man: two doors, two tigers. He had also made known the fate of the escaped bride: death by strangulation. Finally, he had made it clear that his own daughter, though she was the apple of his eye, must pay a price for deceiving him: marriage to the person he chose for her.

The king's steward and his court were aware of his plans and did not approve. They talked privately about what could possibly be done to stop their king. "His Highness has gone too far," the steward said one day. "His plan is nothing short of madness."

"Yes, I agree," responded the constable. "It saddens me to say this but it appears that we are being ruled by a madman. Is there anyone who can get His Majesty to change his mind regarding this situation? We must immediately inform the chancellor of our concerns."

---

27   **entourage** (n) a group of attendants or associates, as of a person of rank or importance

Meanwhile, the Royal Council was meeting in secret to discuss the ways of their king. The Council members were horrified to learn of His Majesty's intentions regarding the young man and the beautiful lady. They also expressed their dismay[28] upon learning of the king's plan for his daughter.

After hours of discussion, the Council members agreed that the king had ruled his kingdom without restraint for far too long, and could not be permitted to carry out the heinous[29] acts of which he had been speaking. "Perhaps it is partly our fault that this has gone on for so long," stated a senior Council member. "We should have intervened[30] long ago."

Pounding his fist on the wooden table, the chancellor ended their meeting with a declaration: "We have always been loyal to our king; however, justice for the subjects of this kingdom must take precedence[31] over loyalty to the throne. His Majesty must be opposed."

---

28   **dismay** (n) disheartenment; disillusionment; alarm
29   **heinous** (adj) terrible, dreadful, monstrous
30   **intervene** (v) to come between disputing people, groups; intercede; mediate
31   **precedence** (n) preference

7
ROYAL FLUSH

The king ordered the young man brought to the arena that very evening. Standing before the twin doors for the second time, the young man felt a cold sweat on his face. *My life is over, but the time with my princess was worth it.* He shuddered, took one last look at his princess, and prepared to meet his end.

A sudden shuffling commotion erupted in the crowd near the king. This caused the young man to turn and face the area in which the king was seated. He saw that a fight seemed to be brewing there. "My God, what is happening?" he asked.

Members of the court, including the king's steward, had taken hold of the king and were dragging him to the center of the arena. Once in front of the double doors, they released the king. "Come with me," the steward said as he grabbed the young man's arm and lead him out of the arena. The crowd watched in horror as this switch was being made.

Hundreds of spectators filled the arena, as was their custom when the king held a trial. Many of the onlookers were loyal to His Majesty, and considered how they could intervene to save their king. However, the constable had placed guards around the amphitheater, preventing spectators from reaching the center of the arena where the king stood.

Now alone in the arena, the king looked around. The Chancellor of the Royal Council announced: "Your Highness, you must refrain from persecuting[32] the young man and your daughter, and accept their matrimony, or you will make the same choice that you would have had the young man make."

The king could not believe his ears. "My daughter will not marry a commoner!" he shouted. "I will never allow that to happen."

"Then choose. Choose now."

"Balderdash!" shouted the king. "I choose neither the left door, nor the right. Now get me out of this arena this instant or I will have all your heads this very day!"

---

32   **persecute** (v) to pursue or harass

Both doors were opened simultaneously, and two tigers entered the arena.

The king yelled, "I said neither the left nor the right, you fools! What have you done?"

"We have given you your wish, Your Majesty. You will not have what is behind one door or the other. Instead you will have what is behind both doors."

The tigers entered the arena. They slowly circled the king, their eyes fixed upon him.

Have they all betrayed me? His Majesty wondered. *This cannot be happening.*

The crowd gasped and trembled as one tiger knocked the king off his feet, a single swipe of his powerful paw crashing into the king's left shoulder. An expression of excruciating[33] pain appeared on his face as His Highness lay sprawled on the ground. He staggered to his feet and looked at the tigers. Their angry eyes and steady growl told the king that his end was near.

Terrified by the scene before him, His Majesty placed his right hand over his pounding heart. Suddenly, the other tiger let out a thunderous roar and pounced on the king. A single piercing scream was heard throughout the arena as the tiger's teeth and claws tore through His Majesty's skin like an axe of one of his henchmen going through the neck of a condemned prisoner. Blood poured out of the king's multiple wounds, staining and saturating the sandy ground around him.

The king's death had been quick. However, the mauling and devouring of his body continued since His Majesty had allowed both tigers to become ravenously hungry for this important trial.

---

33   **excruciating** (adj) unbearable

The crowds' cries and shouts were of no avail.[34] All that was left of His Highness was a bloody mess, and a pile of shredded royal garb, almost unrecognizable. The king's sparkling crown had settled upon the sandy ground of the arena several yards from his remains.

Upon the king's death, iron bells sounded, reverberating[35] throughout the arena, silencing the spectators. The young man saw the tears in the eyes of the princess and held her close. The Chancellor of the Royal Council approached them.

"I am truly sorry, dear princess. Your father has met a most unfortunate end, but one that he has brought upon himself, I'm afraid. And now you must take your rightful place in the palace as the future queen of the land."

Distraught after having witnessed the brutal death of her father, the princess stood in silence, tears rolling down her cheeks. The chancellor bowed his head, giving her a moment to compose herself.

The princess gasped, then took her lover's hand. She turned to face him and said, "If I am to be queen, then you will be king." The young man felt his heart swell with a pride he had never before experienced.

---

34   **avail** (n) advantage; use
35   **reverberate** (v) echo, ring, resonate, vibrate

The chancellor paused, taken aback by the princess' boldness as well as her proposition.[36] Then he bowed to the future royal couple, and announced to the crowd. "Ladies and gentleman, we will soon have a new king and queen."

---

36 **proposition (n)** the act of offering or suggesting something to be considered, accepted, adopted, or done

The crowd was silent at first, too stunned to comprehend the scene before them. Then, slowly, applause began to erupt throughout the crowd, building until it reached an ear-piercing crescendo.[37] A medley of horns sounded, loud and lovely, filling every inch of space in the amphitheater. People began to shout from all around the arena:

"His Highness!"

"Her Majesty!"

"Long live the king and queen."

Coming to terms with her father's death, the future queen wiped the tears from her face. She and the young man embraced, then she turned to face the steward. "My friend, I am simply overwhelmed by all of this," she said. "Your help and advice are needed now more than ever."

"My queen, your father's entire court did not approve of His Majesty's decision to end the life of the young man in such a fashion. Allowing an accused individual the opportunity to make a choice is one thing. Simply throwing him to the lions – or tigers as it were – is another matter entirely. How could we possibly condone[38] such a barbaric[39] practice?"

---

37   **crescendo** (n) buildup, climax
38   **condone** (v) excuse, overlook, tolerate
39   **barbaric** (adj) uncivilized, primitive

The steward continued. "Furthermore, he was planning on having the escaped bride strangled. It was only a matter of time before he would have found her. In fact, several horsemen are searching for her as we speak.

And you, my dear queen, could never have lived your life as you wished as long as your father ruled the kingdom."

8
A NEW DAY

The queen asked the steward to call off the search for the beautiful lady, and so the escaped bride was never found. The church ruled that her marriage to the young man would be annulled[40] immediately because she had abandoned him.

The new king and queen soon married during a lovely but simple ceremony in accordance with the queen's wishes.

---

40   **annul** (v) cancel, terminate, invalidate

The wedding took place outdoors, in the lovely garden in which the couple had first met. Their Royal Council and their court witnessed the ceremony performed by the priest.

The Chancellor of the Royal Council was the first to congratulate the bride and groom after the ceremony. Though he had known of the queen's relationship with the young man for some time, and had understood her desire to be free to choose her own husband, the idea that a commoner would become king had required some contemplation[41] on his part.

Following the wedding, a modest coronation was held in the same garden. Then the Royal Council directed a procession[42] of horses and carriages throughout the kingdom which culminated[43] with the royal couple taking their place in the palace as the new king and queen.

---

41   **contemplation** (n) thought, inspection, consideration
42   **procession** (n) a line of people, animals, vehicles, etc., that move along or proceed in orderly succession or in a formal and ceremonious manner
43   **culminate** (v) end, conclude

Finally, the king and queen, along with their guests, enjoyed a feast in the great hall. A procession of servants entered the room to serve them the magnificent meal that the cooks had prepared which included roasted meat and fish, freshly baked fruit tarts, nuts, fine wine, and delicacies beyond compare.

The king and queen were overjoyed to start their life together, and gradually adapted to their new role as rulers of the kingdom. Their devoted and dutiful steward saw to the couple's every need, as did their court.

The royal couple implemented one change in the kingdom immediately; they put an end to royal trials in the amphitheater. Instead, the king's arena held jousting[44] matches and chariot races to the delight of hundreds of spectators, as well as special musical and theatrical performances given by traveling entertainers.

The new king enjoyed being outdoors as much as he had when he was a courtier. He went on occasional hunting trips in the forest with the men in his court, and hunting dogs soon became a familiar sight around the castle. Also, His Majesty learned to hunt with falcons, impressed by their ability to catch smaller birds and other animals such as rabbits. In addition to these outings with his new companions, the king enjoyed frequent walks in the gardens and the courtyards with his bride, the lovely new queen.

An atmosphere of love and respect pervaded[45] the kingdom and grew stronger with each passing month. At the same time, the hardships that the king and queen had faced early in their relationship eventually faded to a distant memory.

---

44   **jousting** (n) competing, sparring
45   **pervade** (v) to become spread throughout all parts of

One morning, the couple gathered together their court and servants so that the king could make an important announcement. The royal staff clapped and cheered upon learning that he and his beautiful queen were expecting a child.

Season followed season, and soon the royal staff found themselves fussing over a precious baby girl. Nurses took charge of the child, but the king and queen, as well as their court, were all involved in the child's care.

Years passed, and the fair princess grew to be the mirror image of the beautiful queen, in likeness and in spirit. She loved spending time with the children of the castle's servants, who were her dear friends in spite of their parents' status.

Though the princess was still a child, the queen started to contemplate her future. *She is very young,* the queen thought; *yet it is never too early to plan for the day when she will be grown and have a family of her own.*

"Mother, may I have my friends over?" the little princess asked one day. "I would like to play with them."

"My dear sweet child," the queen answered. "Perhaps it is time for you to start associating with other royal children such as yourself."

"Oh, mother, please listen! I must be the one to choose my friends."

The queen stopped suddenly, glancing at her husband and pondering her daughter's words.

Looking at the queen, the king smiled softly, but said nothing.

The queen was silent for a few moments; her mind whirled with memories of all she had been through while courting her own dear husband. *My goodness*, she thought. *Have my father's ways become my own? Will royal bloodlines have a bearing on my daughter's friendships?*

The queen regarded her husband again, then glanced at her daughter who looked up at her, the question still in her eyes. Finally, the queen spoke.

"Ah, I do believe you are right, my dear child. Yes... of course you will choose your own friends. Of course you will."

THE END

9
GLOSSARY

acclimated (v) . . . . . to become accustomed to a new
climate or environment; to adapt

annul (v) . . . . cancel, terminate, invalidate

avail (n) . . . . advantage; use

avarice (n) . . . . insatiable greed for riches; miserly
desire to gain and hoard wealth

banish (v) . . . . send away, drive out

barbaric (adj) . . . . . uncivilized, primitive

burly (adj) . . . . large in bodily size; stout

condone (v) . . . . excuse, overlook, tolerate

conniving (adj) . . . . scheming, deceitful, devious

constable (n) . . . . . . the commander of all armed forces
in the kingdom

contemplation (n) . . . thought, inspection, consideration

courtier (n) . . . . a person who is part of a ruler's
court, who lives with the ruler and
depends on him for a living

crescendo (n) . . . . . . buildup, climax

culminate (v) . . . . . . end, conclude

dismay (n). . . . . disheartenment; disillusionment; alarm

dissipated (v) . . . . . . dissolved, disintegrated

entourage (n) . . . . . . a group of attendants or associates, as of a person of rank or importance

excruciating (adj). . . unbearable

heinous (adj). . . . . . terrible, dreadful, monstrous

heirloom (n) . . . . . . valuable treasure

henchman (n). . . . . . an unscrupulous supporter or adherent of a political figure or cause, especially one motivated by the hope of personal gain

imperceptible (adj). . undetectable

implore (v) . . . . beg, plead

indisposed (adj) . . . . unwilling, disinclined, reluctant, under the weather

intervene (v). . . . . . to come between disputing people, groups; intercede; mediate

irk (v) . . . . bother, annoy

jousting (n) . . . . competing, sparring

lenient (adj) . . . . tolerant, permissive, indulgent

mourn (v) . . . . to feel or express sorrow or grief

persecute (v) . . . . . . to pursue or harass

pervade (v) . . . . to become spread throughout all parts of

precedence (n) . . . . . preference

procession (n) . . . . . . a line of people, animals, vehicles, etc., that move along or proceed in orderly succession or in a formal and ceremonious manner

proposition (n) . . . . . the act of offering or suggesting something to be considered, accepted, adopted, or done

quiver (v) . . . . to shake with a slight but rapid motion; to tremble

reverberate (v) . . . . . echo, ring, resonate, vibrate

scoundrel (n) . . . . . . a person who is a rascal or a villain

semi- . . . . a prefix meaning half
(A semicircle is half a circle.)

sparsely (adv) . . . . . . lightly, sparingly

stammer (v) . . . . to speak with involuntary breaks and
pauses

steward (n) . . . . a person who manages the daily
affairs of the castle, including its
finances, and is in charge of the
servants

stifling (adj) . . . . stuffy, muggy, airless

stout (adj) . . . . heavy, portly

transpire (v) . . . . to occur; happen; take place

undermine (v) . . . . . challenge, undercut, weaken

wrath (n) . . . . anger, rage, fury

ACKNOWLEDGMENTS

Thank you to Joanne Bergbom, Daniela Bivona, Gary Costarella, Joseph Cuomo, Martha Formato, Julie Johnston, Laraine Rudy, Diane Sismour, and Nancy Slater for sharing their thoughts and insights regarding the publication of this story.

ABOUT THE AUTHOR

Linda Costarella is a reading and special education teacher who enjoys writing fiction, non-fiction, and poetry. She lives in New York with her husband and son.